Moysterings™

A Lowcountry Fable

SUSAN M. LEE

Illustrated by Nanjoo Hong

AuthorHouse™
1663 Liberty Drive
Bloomington, IN 47403
www.authorhouse.com
Phone: 1 (800) 839-8640

This is a work of fiction. All of the characters, names, incidents, organizations, and dialogue in this novel are either the products of the author's imagination or are used fictitiously.

Published by AuthorHouse 11/21/2019

ISBN: 978-1-7283-1065-7 (sc)
ISBN: 978-1-7283-2720-4 (hc)
ISBN: 978-1-7283-1066-4 (e)

Library of Congress Control Number: 2019905990

Print information available on the last page.

This book and its illustrations are works of fiction. Names, characters, places, and incidents either are products of the author's and illustrator's imagination or are used fictitiously. Any resemblance to actual events or locales or persons, living or dead, is entirely coincidental.

This book is printed on acid-free paper.

authorHOUSE®

To my loving family

Thwack, thwack, thwack! Hematop hammered busily at the stony oyster clusters with his long orange, knife-like beak. He was an American Oystercatcher. His stocky feathered body was brown-and-white, and the bright orange rings encircling his eyes stood out in bold contrast to his black head.

It was three o'clock in the afternoon, and the salty marsh known as Gullah Bay was at low tide. The sun was still high, and the day was unseasonably warm for February. From a distance, this intertidal landscape appeared to be dark, barren, and dead. But, as Hematop knew too well, within these undulating crater-like masses thrived an entire universe that was bustling with life and rich with food and nutrients.

Hematop nimbly skipped atop the jagged edges of the tightly packed oyster colonies. Having waited impatiently for low tide, the oystercatcher busied himself. It was time to feed. Now unprotected and exposed, the abundant oyster reefs lay ripe for the picking.

Thwack, thwack, thwack! Hematop attacked the slowly surfacing oyster bed. Suddenly, he perked up his head. In the distance, the bird could hear the rumbling of an approaching dinghy. Steering the small boat was Kudima Diggs, a gentle-faced, bearded, middle-aged dark man. He was dressed in a long-sleeved plaid flannel shirt, weathered blue jeans and rugged waterproof waders. Chalky cakes of mud smudged his clothing, and salt rings spotted his spectacles. Approaching the edge of the mud flats, Kudima simmered the noisy motor down to a bubbling gurgle. Finding his mark, he anchored, shut off the motor, and climbed out onto the mud-packed tract carrying two large white buckets.

Annoyed at the disturbance, Hematop ceased his foraging and watched Kudima work his way around the jagged reefs. While Kudima usually harvested the oysters in a circular pattern, plodding along the outer muddy borders of the reefs, today, he departed from his general routine. With crunching footsteps, Kudima carefully climbed to the middle of one of the largest and tallest mounds. Wearing thick padded gloves, he dug and pried with a blunt knife to dislodge the oysters from their clusters.

Once Kudima had loaded his dinghy with as many oysters as it could hold, he clambered back aboard. The dinghy's rusty motor clanked and sputtered to life, and discharging a smoky trail scented of gasoline, Kudima departed.

"Stinky noisy boats," sniffed Hematop as he quickly skipped to the top of the oyster reef that Kudima had just harvested. "But no matter, he has made my task easier for me."

Peering down, Hematop's orange-ringed eyes widened, and his beak curled with a smile of appreciation. "Look at these tremendous oysters that have been hiding deep within this reef!" Spying a particularly gigantic oyster, indeed the largest oyster that he had ever encountered, Hematop *wheep*ed in delight and immediately began knocking on the large oyster's massive shell.

Thwack, thwack, thwack, the bird's bill sounded against the hard oyster shell. Suddenly, a loud yet muffled sound responded. Jerking his head up, the startled bird stood still. Silence. *Thwack, thwack, thwack,* the bird continued, but the muffled sound returned, more loudly this time. Completely bemused, the bird stopped again. Once more, the sounds stopped. Peering around, Hematop quickly scanned the area. Only the tall and lanky great blue heron was quietly foraging nearby.

I must be hearing things, thought Hematop. Looking back down and admiring his prize oyster, he grinned again. He returned to hammering away at the shell when, suddenly, a strong jet of salt water squirted from the oyster, stinging and blinding Hematop in his right orange-rimmed eye.

"*Wheep, wheep, wheep!*" the startled bird exclaimed, bouncing backward with his wings aflutter.

"What is wrong with you?!" bellowed the oyster, his shell wide open and revealing two bulging eyes that glared under deeply furrowed brows. "Don't you understand the meaning of 'No one is home'?"

"What? You speak?" spluttered Hematop. His long orange bill dropped open in astonishment.

"Of course, I speak. Why wouldn't I?" the oyster retorted, his gelatinous form quivering with irritation.

"Why?" stammered the incredulous bird. "Because you are an *oyster!* Why, you are among the lowest in the food chain!" Regaining his composure, he blustered, "You are of inferior rank!"

"Inferior rank!?" thundered the large oyster, his mass billowing out like a sail caught in a gust of wind. "And look who is speaking, a low-life bird that only knows to hammer away, badgering our peaceful oyster reefs. Why, you have no fishing skills or hunting finesse."

The bird's immediate response was to angrily lunge at the belligerent and insulting oyster. But the oyster quickly shut his rock-like shell in time to block the bird's ferocious assault. Enraged, Hematop began to hammer more emphatically until another piercing jet of water squirted and blinded his left eye. The bird pitched backward as he screeched, flapping his wings haphazardly, his left eye now closed and stinging.

"Stop! Stop!" yelled the oyster. "Give me a moment's truce!"

"Huh?" spluttered the bird, his left eye still twitching.

"I will tell you a riddle. If you cannot guess the correct answer, then you shall leave me be," the oyster stoutly propositioned.

"A riddle?" parroted Hematop, his head jerking backward. Stupefied, he paused, but after a moment's contemplation, he narrowed both eyes, cocked his head, and asked, "If I answer the riddle correctly, what do I get in return?"

"I shall not resist, but shall open my doors and give you free entrance," heaved the oyster resignedly.

"Yes, but why should I bargain with you over a riddle," sneered the bird, "when you offer nothing more than I can get on my own without the need of a pact?"

"Because," rebutted the oyster, "it may not only save my life, but *yours* as well."

Intrigued and almost humored, Hematop could not resist.

"Save *my* life? Wheee-hee-hee-hee, that's a joke," the bird chortled. "You, who is anchored on this reef with nowhere to go, and who is my big prize for the day, should say that my life is at risk? Wheee-hee-hee-hee! Okay, it's a deal. Tell me your riddle!"

Naturally, Hematop had no intention of keeping to this agreement, but he was curious to hear the riddle all the same.

Unbeknownst to Hematop, the large oyster had been eyeing a dark speck flying high in the distant sky, its form growing more prominent as it circled downward in its slow and majestic glide.

"What, Master Oystercatcher, is dark brown with a white head and tail, soars high, and has a killer grip?" the oyster asked, trying to keep a straight expression. All the while, he looked past Hematop's face, watching the approaching flight of the larger bird.

"Huh?" *wheep*ed Hematop. "That's your riddle? How in the blue skies am I to answer that?"

"Do you give up?" demanded the oyster.

"No, why should I give up?" shrieked Hematop.

"Because, dear sir, you have run out of time and will soon be eaten by the answer. Beware, for the answer is the bald eagle!" The large oyster's body pulsed forward, pointing to the sky behind Hematop.

Twisting in the direction that the oyster pointed, Hematop turned in time to hear a piercing *kak-kak-kak* and see the rapid advance of an enormous and fierce bald eagle. Its broad, mighty wings extended wide, and its deadly bright-yellow talons were outstretched and reaching forward in full attack mode.

"*Whee-ah, whee-ah, whee-ah!*" screeched Hematop, stumbling and thrashing his wings in fear. Quickly righting himself, he frantically flew off the reef in the opposite direction just as the bald eagle swooshed past. The mighty eagle's powerful talons dipped just below the surface of a nearby shallow pool. Grabbing a large fish with its death grip, the magnificent bird soared back up into the sky.

The large oyster jeered and blew raspberries at the diminishing figure of the fleeing oystercatcher before sinking back into his shell.

"Phew, that was too close!" he sighed. His entire body deflated into an exhausted puddle, and his shell hung half-closed as if on broken hinges.

The nearby great blue heron had been silently watching with astonishment at the discourse between Hematop and the oyster. Noiselessly, he loped over to the oyster reef.

Clearing his throat, the tall gray-blue bird softly croaked, "Dear sir, I beg your pardon, but I could not help overhearing your conversation with the oystercatcher. You should not be so offended that he was surprised that you spoke."

At the sound of the remark, the oyster tensed and his mantle puckered. However, upon seeing the heron, he relaxed for this tall bird was no predator to his kind.

"And why should I not be offended?" the oyster ballooned. "That impudent bird vexed me with his scurrilous mischaracterizations! Yes, my kind may be among the lowest in the food chain, but that does not make us *inferior!* No, it does not. Indeed, we play a vital role in this aquatic chain, for without us, you could not exist."

"It is here from our oyster reefs that the chain of life begins. We are the fertile seeds of existence. Each of our females scatters the waters with millions of eggs, which are feed for the small marine critters. And our reefs provide safe shelter to the young sea creatures so that they can grow and procreate before being consumed by bigger fish, which in turn are eaten by larger fish, which in continued succession are preyed upon by even greater fish that ultimately are devoured by predators such as you."

"No, without us, you could not exist. You would starve!" the oyster defiantly concluded, folding his arms and pouting out his lower lip.

"Yes, but dear Mr. Oyster, I am sure that the oystercatcher meant no insult," the tall bird placated. "Perhaps he was gobsmacked that you spoke at all. Indeed, in my fifteen years of scouting these grounds, I have never heard an oyster speak before."

"Why ever would you think we would wish to speak to any of you?" harrumphed the oyster. Then, somewhat sarcastically, he added, "Ooohhh, I see your rationale ... because we choose not to speak to you, therefore we must not be able to speak at all?"

The dark plumes on the bird's head involuntarily rose to standing points, casting an ominous and regal shadow upon the reef. Stunned by the pure and direct logic of the large oyster's admonishment, the blue heron felt ashamed of his own shallow deduction.

Vigorously shaking his long, shaggy neck in an effort to cast off his embarrassment, the blue heron willed his luxurious plumes to smooth down. Clearing his throat again with a *kraak, kraak, kraak,* the gangling bird said, "Perhaps we started off on the wrong foot. Forgive my rudeness and oversight in not introducing myself. I am Sir Croker of the great blue heron clan. It is my greatest pleasure to make your acquaintance." Placing one lanky leg forward and gallantly folding one wing to his breast, Sir Croker bowed, his sinuous neck sweeping down so his eyes came level with the oyster's.

"And I am Preechuh Kamba Osiituh," the oyster solemnly nodded in return, his chest inflated to its fullest. "I am a Zydn'n Elduh, which is a Grand Master Teacher and keeper of the moysterings. You may call me Mass Kamba."

"Well, it is my honor to know you, Mass Kamba," the tall bird acknowledged, bowing low again. Then, lifting his face close to the oyster's, Sir Croker softly inquired, "But, I beg your pardon, may I ask, what are moysterings?"

"Moysterings are the murmurs and whisperings of legends passed down through generations of oyster reefs. They are stories of ancient remembrance," Mass Kamba explained. "Our reefs encompass the full cycle of life, for they constitute our graveyard and our birthplace. Because I am one of the designated Zydn'n Elduhs, it is imperative that I am protected so that our moysterings are preserved. Our children, which we call little spatlings, instinctively know to anchor upon us elders. They learn our teachings and protect us with cover so that we can survive and pass on our legends."

Sadly lowering his eyes, the oyster grimaced and continued, "I had no choice but to break our reef silence and speak with that pesky oystercatcher. My colony was harvested earlier today by the dark man. It is most lamentable, for many of my finest pupils were stripped away from me, and now I am exposed and vulnerable. I had to deflect the bird's attack. I am, however, afraid that I will not be able to avert future danger."

"Let's face it," the oyster wryly smiled, "How many times will a bald eagle swoop by with such absolute perfect timing?"

Wonderstruck, Sir Croker inhaled deeply. He was overwhelmed to discover that such erudite dynasties thrived within these reefs.

"Yes, I can appreciate your concern," he sympathized. "And now I understand why you are such a mammoth oyster. You are the largest oyster I have ever seen."

"Of course I am," Mass Kamba said, standing erect. "I am nearly eighty years old."

Seeing that this comment brightened the sad oyster's spirits somewhat, Sir Croker offered, "Well, my dear friend, I would be happy to remain here with you for the rest of this day and ward off any predators."

"Oh, thank you, Sir Croker, I would be much obliged," Mass Kamba gushed, bowing deeply. "Truly I would. Thank you, thank you."

So to help pass the time away, Mass Kamba shared several moysterings of old with the attentive and spellbound blue heron. He recounted the days of many moons ago, when dark-skinned men dressed scantily in deer hides would paddle to the oyster reefs in long, narrow canoes.

How, one day, large wooden ships came to these waters, filled with pale-skinned men adorned in brightly colored silks and gilded in heavy metal armor and helmets. Mass Kamba spoke of the many shipwrecks that destroyed entire oyster colonies.

But these catastrophes did not stop the ships from coming to these waters, and then many more ships from distant horizons arrived, bringing more pale-faced people. He told of the wars between the pale-skinned men, of their bloody and violent battles, and of the great fires that could be seen burning upon the land.

Then Mass Kamba recited the moysterings of the Gullah, when the big ships suddenly stopped coming to these shores and a new era of peace and tranquility blessed the waters. During this period, gentle and peaceful dark-skinned people fished the waters and sang melodic songs.

Utterly captivated by Mass Kamba's eloquent recitation of the reef's moysterings, Sir Croker snuggled into a resting squat, his long, slender neck folding into his body. And the hours and minutes pleasantly and swiftly ticked away. Their conversation paused only when the two congenial creatures turned to face the beautiful sunset, breathing in the remaining warmth of the departing sun.

"Such a glorious sundown," murmured Mass Kamba, contentedly sprinkling out gentle streams of water.

"Hmm, yes, indeed," hummed Sir Croker in reply. "I have traveled to many places far and near and have seen many a sunset, but none as beautiful as here."

"How wonderful it must be to see beyond our beaches, and to travel far and wide," gurgled Mass Kamba.

Alarmed at the sudden change in Mass Kamba's voice, Sir Croker looked down to see the large oyster nearly covered in water. So engrossed had the heron been with the bewitching sunset that he had not noticed the nearly imperceptible rising of the water level and the creeping return of high tide.

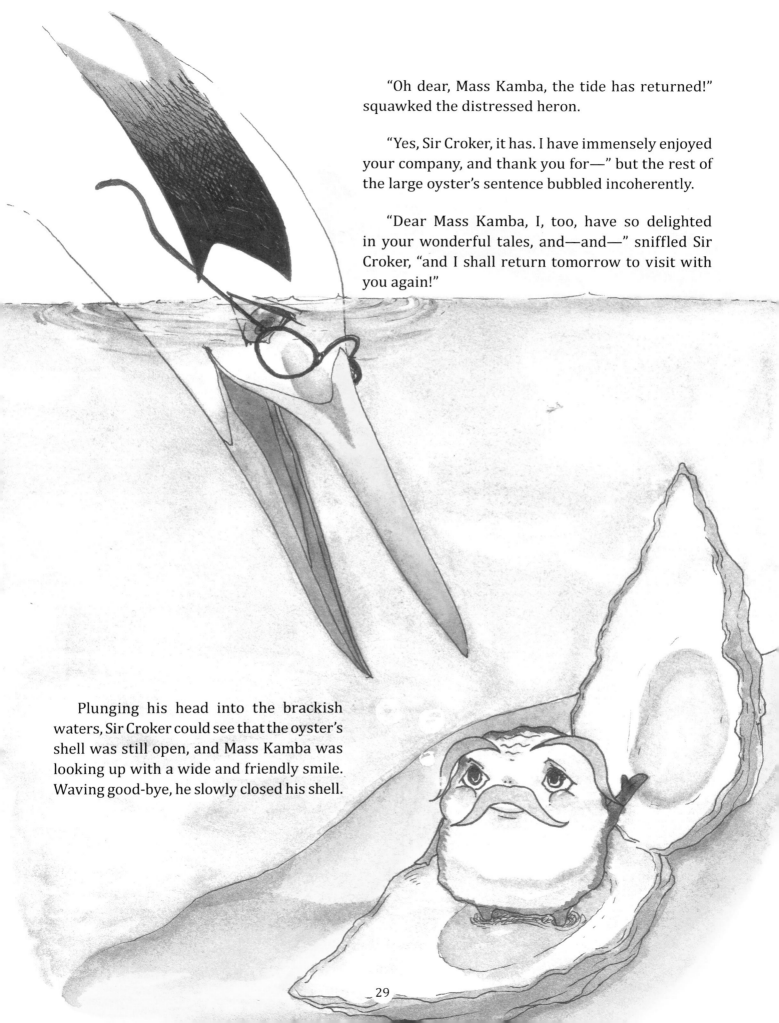

"Oh dear, Mass Kamba, the tide has returned!" squawked the distressed heron.

"Yes, Sir Croker, it has. I have immensely enjoyed your company, and thank you for—" but the rest of the large oyster's sentence bubbled incoherently.

"Dear Mass Kamba, I, too, have so delighted in your wonderful tales, and—and—" sniffled Sir Croker, "and I shall return tomorrow to visit with you again!"

Plunging his head into the brackish waters, Sir Croker could see that the oyster's shell was still open, and Mass Kamba was looking up with a wide and friendly smile. Waving good-bye, he slowly closed his shell.

Lifting his head out with a splash, Sir Croker's eyes anxiously scoured the nearby shores. "A landmark, I must find and remember a landmark so that I can return again tomorrow," the bird panted. "There, yes, there."

In the distance, a white motorboat with blue trimmings was hoisted upon a rickety pier, and mounted upon one of the pier's pilings was a tattered flag that waved gently in the breeze. "Yes, I shall commit this to my memory, and return again tomorrow." And, with this conviction and the vision of the boat firmly embedded in his mind, Sir Croker opened his broad wings and with slow, powerful beats lifted into the darkening sky.

The next day, during early morning high tide on the other side of the island, Sir Croker voraciously foraged along the white sandy beaches. With his long yellow blade-like bill, the heron impaled his prey, gulping the fish down whole. He was ravenous, since he had not eaten during his long discourse with Mass Kamba. The tall bird eagerly ate as much as his hunting could yield so he could devote the rest of the afternoon to visiting with the sage old oyster. Measuring the high level of the ocean with its strong currents, the tall bird knew that the oyster reefs must be bustling with activity. He envisioned Mass Kamba, fully submerged, feeding on the plentiful free-floating plankton.

Once the sun rose to the highest point in the sky, Sir Croker flew westward, toward the mudflats and shallow marshes. Returning to Gullah Bay, the blue heron recognized the pier that held the white boat with blue trim, and he gracefully landed on a tall wood piling speckled with soft sand and smelling of the rich salt waters. Here Sir Croker perched, languidly stretching out his large wings and tipping his long beak up toward the bright sky. Sunning himself, the contented bird patiently waited for low tide.

The marine marsh had totally transformed from the dark crater-like terrain of the day before. The tide was still high, and the panoramic marsh was now an open expanse of calm, rippling dark-green waters that shimmered silver in the sunlight. There were no traces of the vast oyster colonies sequestered below.

But, as time tiptoed by, the marsh waters slowly receded, peeling away as the tips of the oyster reefs began to surface. Before long, in keeping with ancient tidal patterns, the undulating silhouette of countless oyster reefs re-emerged.

Squinting, Sir Croker reconnoitered the landscape, now filled with endless mounds of dark oyster reefs. Then he spied an oystercatcher noisily banging away at a particularly tall oyster bed. With great urgency, the heron took flight and began barking his loud warning call. *"Fraunk! Fraunk! Fraunk!"* He swooped down upon the orange-billed invader. The oystercatcher had never been hounded by a great blue heron before. Spooked, he hastily flew away.

Turning around to view the pier, Sir Croker tilted his head and surmised, "Yes, this angle looks familiar. Yes, yes, I must be on the correct spot."

"Hello? Dear Mass Kamba, it is I, Sir Croker," the tall bird called. "I have returned to visit with you again."

But there was no response.

"Master Grand Teacher, I have returned to thank you for your stories."

Again, there was only silence.

"My dear friend, please join me in another conversation," Sir Croker sighed sadly. "I have never had such a captivating discourse such as ours, and I have come to share with you my stories. For, unlike you, who have the treasure of history and knowledge passed down through centuries of your ancestors, I have the gift of flight and travel. I have seen things that your forebearers could not. I can share with you the views of the dry land and of this present day. You can absorb this knowledge and pass it on to your communities and your future children."

"I am here, Sir Croker," came the muffled voice of Mass Kamba, "and, if you don't mind, please, you are standing on me."

"Oh, dear!" piped the tall bird, jumping a step back. "A million apologies, my friend. I was afraid I wouldn't ... why ... ?" Sir Croker stopped mid-sentence. His yellow eyes widened with astonishment, for the large oyster's appearance had changed beyond recognition. His large, craggy shell was now encrusted with at least a dozen new little spats.

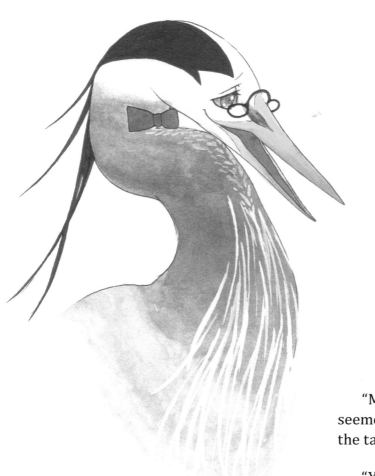

"Mass Kamba, you look so different. You seemed to have acquired some new neighbors," the tall bird observed quizzically.

"Yes, an emergency alert was issued last night," beamed Mass Kamba, "and these young spatlings came rushing to my aid. They are my new pupils."

"That is such wonderful news," smiled the good-natured Sir Croker. "I thought perhaps today I would share with you some of my journeys. Would you like that?"

"Yes, yes, oh yes!" chorused the child-like voices of the spatlings, their little shells rapidly opening and clapping shut.

"Ha-ha-ha, looks like the majority rules," the large oyster chuckled jovially.

Pleasantly surprised by the unexpected audience, Sir Croker was delighted and felt an immediate affection for these darling little oysters. "Well, then, where shall we begin?" And with that, the gentle bird folded his tall, lean frame into a comfortable resting squat and began sharing his stories.

Sir Croker described the dry lands and recounted how large portions of the island, once lush and thick with trees, were cut down and replaced with endless streets and countless big structures. The bird spoke of the enumerable people of different skin colors who inhabited the dry lands and lived in the large buildings. He painted a night image of twinkling lights, which he called land stars. As Sir Croker spoke, the little spatlings *ooh*ed and *aah*ed, and soft intermittent murmurs hummed from other parts of the reef.

And, while the oysters were familiar with boats, they learned of new and different types of moving vehicles, such as cars, motorbikes, and buses. These, Sir Croker explained, transported people from one destination to another, and large planes carried people high into the skies.

"Yes, yes, we have seen these planes fly by!" chirped the spatlings in unison.

And so the lovely afternoon passed in this enjoyable and entertaining fashion. But, as time would have it, the sunset arrived along with the inevitable high tide. However, Sir Croker was more attentive to it this time, for the great bird did not want to suffer another hasty and incomplete parting.

So, with ample time, the friendly and happy creatures showered each other with many gracious compliments, and the spatlings enthusiastically thanked Sir Croker for his tales. Bowing deeply again to the venerable Mass Kamba, who bowed solemnly back in return, the noble bird took his leave, promising again to return the next day.

But when the heron returned the following afternoon, the white boat with blue trim was nowhere to be found. Without this landmark, all the piers looked the same. For hours, Sir Croker flew above, landing on one oyster reef after another, hoarsely calling out to Mass Kamba. But the increasingly desperate and sad heron received no reply. At nightfall, downtrodden and grieved, Sir Croker flew away.

Under the dark, shallow waters, Mass Kamba, now covered with even more spatlings, was deep in the meditation of moysterings. He recounted how the great blue heron had saved his life, and he transcribed the bird's tales. Soon, these new stories were transmitted by murmurs and whisperings throughout the oyster kingdom and, over time, became known as the Great Blue Heron Legend.

Above the waters, a dry-land legend was also born. It was told by the oysterman, Kudima Diggs. He spoke of an old heron that, until the end of its days, appeared in Gullah Bay at every low tide. Croaking a melancholy lament, this crazed old bird guarded the oyster reefs. It chased away the oystercatchers, and it screamed and swooped down at him whenever he tried to harvest the oysters. Eventually, Kudima Diggs abandoned the bay and did not return until the old bird had long passed on.

<u>Author's Note:</u> *Kudima* is Gullah for "to work or hoe"; *Mass* is Gullah for "master" when associated with a name; *Kamba* is African Luba for "ancestor" or Gullah for "grave"; *Croker* is a Gullah nickname; *Zydn'n Elduh* is Gullah for "presiding elder." *Preechuh* is Gullah for "preacher"; and *Osiituh* is Gullah for "oyster."

<u>Author's Note to Educators:</u> This lyrical fable was written with no specific age group in mind. Although, at first blush, one would categorize it as a children's book because of its personified fictional characters, it is intended to be enjoyed by readers of all ages. For that reason, I resisted numerous syntax and vocabulary recommendations to scale down the prose. The English language is resplendent, brimming with an opulent array of vocabulary. One can peruse among a treasure trove of slightly varying words, searching until one finds the perfect word with the subtle nuance that fully expresses an action, a moment, an emotion or a thought. It is this cache of wonderful words that is being lost with today's over-simplification of the English language. Much research has gone into writing this little tale. It was written with the educators in mind – to provide a sounding board for young students to discuss Lowcountry history, wetland ecosystems and marine life, ornithology, Gullah culture, and, yes, vocabulary.

Behind the Scenes.

Susan's initial illustrations of Mass Kamba and Sir Croker

About the Author

A graduate of Boston University College of Communications and Columbia Law School, Susan Lee practiced New York and New Jersey law for nearly 20 years before she first visited Hilton Head Island, SC. She was instantly enamored with the Lowcountry region -- finding it rich with history, local culture, marine coastal nature, and gorgeous weather. For a wonderful five years, Susan resided in Hilton Head Island before returning back to New Jersey where all her family resides. She dedicates this fable to Hilton Head Island as an expression of her appreciation for the inspiration it breathed into her imagination. Susan can be reached at Moysterings@gmail.com.

About the Illustrator

Nanjoo Hong received her bachelor's degree in fine arts and graphic design from the University of Florida's New World School of the Arts. Her areas of concentration include colors, shapes, and patterns. Nanjoo is currently a graphic designer at the Henry M. Jackson Foundation, a global nonprofit organization headquartered in the Washington, DC metro area. In 2018, she received four awards from Graphic Design USA for Best In-House Design. To illustrate "Moysterings," Nanjoo visited Susan at Hilton Head Island for a week-long research session of full immersion – exploring the beautiful landscape of the Lowcountry with long walks on its beaches, marshland and marine forests. Armed with high-powered binoculars, together with Susan, they would crouch behind bushes as they quietly observed the Great Blue herons, and, of course, watch with amazement at the daily emergence and disappearance of the magnificent tideland oyster colonies. Nanjoo can be reached at NanjooHong.com.

Printed in the United States
By Bookmasters